READ ALL OF THE
BLONDIE MCGHEE MYSTERIES

#1 At Your Service
#2 Hidden in Plain Sight
#3 Growing Suspicion

And coming soon
#4 Pressure to Perform

BLONDIE McGHEE

Growing Suspicion
#3

Ashley Eneriz

Contents

CHAPTER ONE

ROCK, PAPER, SCISSORS

"I will not get in trouble when I solve a crime," I say with my right hand raised. My mother makes me repeat this phrase every morning after I finish breakfast. If you asked me, it's getting kind of old. A girl falls through the school attic and suddenly she's treated like someone with a mug shot.

"Now tell me I'm the best dad ever," my dad chimes in.

"You're the best dad ever," I say with a monotone voice.

"Come on, say it with some oomph," my dad laughs. I clap my hands and raise them over my head energetically. "You are the best D-A-D ever!" I shout trying to sound like a cheerleader.

"Much better," he laughs. "You've earned your first clue to what we will be doing this weekend." He hands me an envelope.

Excitedly I rip it open and pull out a piece of paper. The paper reads,

"Rock, paper, scissors,

Chameleons, toads and ---"

"Huh?" I say after I read it to myself.

"Can you guess the blank?" my dad asks.

"Frogs?" I say unsure.

My dad slaps his hand on his forehead. "It's like you aren't even trying. Think of it as a rhyme. That's the only hint I'm going to give you. "

I read the clue again. *What rhymes with scissors?* My mind draws a blank.

"Blondie, Blondie is a detective, but if she is good is rather objective," my sister, Jana, sings out.

"Jana," my mother says sternly while washing the dishes.

"Nice rhyme and usage of a word, but meanness is something this family can't afford," my dad says with a smirk.

"Nice one, honey," my mom calls out, and she makes her way to my dad. They both raise their hand above their head.

"Oh no, not the..." Jana begins to say.

Too late. My parents enthusiastically high-five each other.

"High five," Jana grumbles as she finishes her sentence.

My parents laugh and Jana shakes her head and looks down at the floor.

Jana acts like this a lot. My mom says it's just her being a teenager. Whatever that means. Though I do have to admit that my parents high five each other a lot. Usually in public.

Last night they high-fived loudly after they ordered the same type of pizza slice from Vince's Pizzeria. I'm pretty sure everyone in the restaurant saw.

"So, Blondie, are you going to take another crack at your clue?" my dad asks.

I hold up the paper again and read the clue out loud.

"Rock, paper, scissors, chameleons, toads, and," I pause trying to think.

"Lizards?" I guess.

"Yes!" My dad shouts enthusiastically. "Great job, sweetheart."

"But what does that even mean?" I ask confused, still looking at the clue.

"Looks like you will have to wait until tomorrow for your next clue."

"Are we going to catch lizards?" I ask curiously.

"You'll see," my dad laughs.

"I bet Blondie will figure out her surprise before the end of the day," my mom says, putting her hand on my shoulder.

"We will see about that," my dad smirks. "I am the clue master, after all."

CHAPTER TWO

BROWNIES AND B MINUSES

As my fourth-grade class and I shuffle into the classroom, Mrs. Clemmons is nowhere in sight. Other kids are starting to notice the same thing, and a few kids shout out, "Where's Mrs. Clemmons?"

"Is she sick?" someone else asks.

"Should we ask the office?" another kid asks.

I look at the board to see if Mrs. Clemmons has given us instructions, but the board is still covered with yesterday's math problems. *That is weird.* Mrs. Clemmons always cleans the board before she leaves school for the day.

Before anyone can ask any more questions, Mrs. Clemmons walks through the classroom door. She is sweaty and quite pale looking.

"Good morning, class," she says trying to sound enthusiastic, but it is obvious that she is out of breath.

"Everyone take your seat and pull out your journals."
Everyone does what she says, but I can't help staring at her.

"Mrs. Clemmons," I say as I raise my hand.

"Yes, Blondie?"

"Are you feeling okay?"

"Oh, yes. Nothing to worry about."

I continue to watch her as she sits down at her desk.

"Oh brownies!" she exclaims.

I follow her gaze to her desk and sure enough, there was a big plate of brownies sitting on her desk. How could I have missed them? Obviously, my detective skills needed some sharpening.

"There is no note. Who was nice enough to bring me brownies?" Mrs. Clemmons asks.

All the kids look around the room, but no one raises their hand.

"Well, thank you to whoever brought the brownies. They look delicious. Let's get started with our morning journal prompt," she says as she walks over to the board.

"What would you do if someone was chasing you?" she says as she writes the prompt on the board.

That's a strange prompt, but what hasn't been strange about this morning?

If I thought Mrs. Clemmons' writing prompt was strange, then I wasn't ready for the rest of the morning. Not only did she forget what 100 divided by 20 was, but then she called Owen by the name of Bradley. We don't even have a Bradley in our class!

Thank goodness for recess! I pulled my dad's clue out of my pocket.

"Rock, paper, scissors, chameleons, toads, and lizards," I say out loud. I wrote in the word "lizards" where the blank was, but that didn't seem to help. *It still doesn't make any sense.*

I spot Bray on the swing set and walk over to her. Bray has been in my class since last year, but we never hung out until this weekend. Her mom is friends with my mom, which means they arranged a get together for us without even asking either of us.

It's not that I didn't want to hang out with Bray, it is just I've never been good at making friends. Usually, I just sit by myself at lunch and read or write in my detective notebook.

But it turns out that Bray and I have a lot of things in common. Sure, she likes soccer and enjoys camping with her family (both I would never be caught dead doing), but we both love reading Nancy Drew and have great taste in music.

"Hey Bray," I wave as I get closer to the swing set.

"Hey there, Blondie. Want to have a swing race?" she asks.

"Maybe in a little bit. First, I need your help solving a mystery."

"Ooh! Just like Sherlock!" Bray squeals, slowing down her swing.

"Sort of," I grin.

I hand her the piece of paper and watch her lips move as she reads it.

"Huh?" she says handing back the paper. "I don't get it. What's the mystery?"

"My dad said we are doing something this weekend, but he won't tell me what. He just gave me this clue, and he says there is going to be another one tomorrow. I'm trying to figure it out before then."

"I'm beat," says Bray. "But if you need help tracking down a missing dog, I'm your girl."

"Thanks, Watson," I laugh.

"Now how about that swing race?" she asks, already pumping her legs wildly.

"Hey, no fair," I call, hopping on the swing, trying to catch up with her.

Before I can catch up to her, though, the recess bell rings.

"Next time I will beat you," I laugh, slowing down my swing.

"We'll see about that," she adds laughing.

As we walk towards the rest of the class, I whisper, "Did you notice anything odd with Mrs. C?"

"Odd? Like what?" she asks.

"You know like how she was late and sweaty this morning. Or how she forgot one hundred divided by twenty."

"She's probably just having an off day," Bray replies.

"But what if something else is going on?" I ask.

"Don't try to make a mystery out of nothing like you always do," Bray laughs.

Before I can say anything, our class starts to walk from the playground to the classroom. *What did she mean make a mystery out of nothing like I always do?*

As we walk in I notice that a huge bite is taken out of one of the brownies on Mrs. Clemmons' desk. I can't wait until I am a grown-up and can eat brownies before lunch time.

"Class, let's get out our grammar books and work on diagraming a few sentences," Mrs. Clemmons says.

She seems to be looking like normal. Maybe this morning was all in my head.

Mrs. Clemmons starts writing, "The large man walks his dog," on the board, but before she can put a period at the end of her sentence she looks at the class.

Her pale face is back, and I spot a bead of sweat dripping down her temple.

"Owen, pass out everyone's book reports," she yells, pointing at a pile of papers on her desk.

Before she can say anything else, she covers her mouth with her hands and runs out of the classroom.

Bray looks at me, and I mouth, "Brownies," while pointing towards Mrs. Clemmons' desk.

Bray's eyes grow wide.

What would Nancy Drew do in this situation?

Aha! A sample!

I dig out my detective kit from my backpack and carefully pull out two plastic bags. Detective Lesson 84: If you are ever without an evidence kit, two sandwich bags will do the trick. Just make sure they are clean. Use one for your hand so that you don't contaminate the evidence.

I look around to see if anyone is watching me, but everyone is either talking or looking at their book report.

Detective lesson 103: Blend into your surroundings. Pretend you aren't doing anything at all, and no one will suspect you.

I quickly walk up to Mrs. Clemmons' desk, pluck a large chunk of the brownie and shove it in the other plastic bag. I hear a gasp behind me.

I turn around quickly.

It is only Bray. She sits closest to Mrs. Clemmons' desk.

"Shh!" I say, holding my finger to my lips. "It's for evidence."

Bray nods with a smile.

I shove the brownie bag into my backpack. I don't know of any testing labs that would test the substance of the brownie, but it never hurts to be prepared.

"Uh-oh," I hear a voice say.

I sit up quickly. *Did someone else see me?*

Owen stands in front of my desk waving a book report in front of my face.

"Looks like Blondie is not as smart as she thinks she is," Owen taunts.

I grab the report from him, but before I can think of a witty comeback, my mouth drops open when I see the large, red B- on the top of my report.

"What?" I say hoarsely, flipping through my report. On the grading sheet, I had gotten good comments on everything, except for the cover. I had drawn my cover myself, which I admit wasn't amazing, but that was because I wasn't a great artist. However, she did say that we couldn't use the computer to make our covers. We had to freehand everything.

I look over at Mark's report and see an A- on top of his paper. His cover was obviously made with the computer. There was even a picture of promo poster from the movie version of the book.

"It's not fair. I don't get it," I say to myself. I slump down in my chair and cross my arms.

My anger doesn't last long once I see that Mrs. Clemmons has returned.

"Sorry about that class. I think I ate too many brownies," she laughs. "Let's finish our grammar lesson."

The brownies!

I pull out my detective notebook and begin writing down all the details from this morning. It is always important to write down everything you think is relevant to your case. This is such an important lesson to remember, because trust me, you will forget small details. And sometimes small details are what solve the case.

CHAPTER THREE

FALSE ACCUSATIONS

As I enter the classroom the next morning, I notice the brownies are gone. *Good thing I got that sample.*

Mrs. Clemmons looks better than she did yesterday. In fact, she looks like nothing happened to her at all.

I guess that mystery is solved, and dad forgot to give me another clue this morning, so his mystery is on hold. Being a detective means that sometimes you have a lot of cases, and sometimes you have a dry season.

"Who can tell me how to solve the problem of three cubed?" Mrs. Clemmons asks, interrupting my thoughts.

I raise my hand.

"Yes, Blondie. Please come solve the problem."

I write out, "3 x 3 x 3," on the board, but before I can write anymore, Mrs. Clemmons yells, "Boys!"

I turn to see who she is talking to.

"The paper please," Mrs. Clemmons says, holding her hand out towards Owen and Samir.

Samir reluctantly hands over the paper, looking down at his desk.

Mrs. Clemmons smooths out the crumpled paper and reads it out loud, "Mrs. C is going to get it."

Mrs. Clemmons looks confused.

"Did you boys write this?" she asks.

Both boys shake their heads.

"Just tell the truth. You won't get in trouble," Mrs. Clemmons says, now in a nicer tone.

Owen's voice squeaks, "We didn't write it. We promise. I just found the paper ball under my desk and..."

"And?" Mrs. Clemmons asks.

"I threw it," Owens whispers.

"Next time you boys decide to make a mess in the classroom, you will stay in from recess and clean it. Understand?"

Owen nods enthusiastically. He is probably excited because he isn't being sent to the office for the second time this month.

I turn back to the board and finish solving the problem.

"Great job, Blondie. Let's try a slightly harder problem," Mrs. Clemmons says, writing above my work.

As I walk back to my seat, I feel a hand bump into mine. Lydia looks at me and forces a small piece of paper in my hand.

Is she seriously trying to pass me a note after Owen and Samir just got in trouble?

I stuff my hand in my pocket just to make sure Mrs. Clemmons doesn't see me.

Once I sit down, I vow not to read the note until lunch, but after only a few minutes of sitting there, I can't help but slip my hand into my pocket to pull out the paper.

Perhaps she has a mystery she wants me to solve.

I carefully unwrap the paper and see, "I know it was you who wrote that note to Mrs. C, and I'm going to tell her at lunch."

It was scribbled in red writing. I look at Lydia, but when I do, she frowns at me and turns her attention to the board.

"Lydia, I didn't write that note," I call out to her when she enters the courtyard with her cafeteria tray.

"Too late, I already told Mrs. C," she shrugs.

"But why would you do that?" I ask.

"Because of what you said yesterday."

"Yesterday? I didn't say anything yesterday!"

"Mhmm!" Lydia nods her head excitedly.

"You said, 'Mrs. Clemmons isn't fair and that she is going to get it."

"Now you are just making up stories," I accuse her.

"Am not!" She says, angrily. "You didn't get an A on your book report, and you were mad."

My jaw drops. *Oh, yes, I remember now. But did I really say those words?*

I scratch my head, trying to remember what exactly I said.

"Are you sure I didn't say, 'It's not fair, I don't get it?'" I ask.

"Don't try to look innocent now."

"I'm just trying to tell you what I really said," I say defensively.

"I know what I saw," she adds.

"What did you see?"

"You were mad about your grade, then you wrote something down in that diary of yours, and then I watched you go to Mrs. Clemmons' desk."

I stay quiet, trying to remember everything I did after I looked at my book report.

"Like I said, it's too late," she says and walks towards the furthest table in the lunch courtyard.

I set my sandwich down and think.

Should I approach Mrs. Clemmons first? Or is that what guilty people do?

Maybe she didn't even believe Lydia's story. Lydia does have a record for telling tall tales. Just last week she told everyone that Owen could transform into a mouse. True, Owen did convince her that it was true. But come on, if you can fall for one of Owens lies that easily, then you are not a credible witness.

I'm so distracted by my thoughts that I don't see Bray sit next to me.

"Hello, earth to Blondie," she laughs, waving her hand in front of my face.

I look at her stunned. "Oh, hi, sorry," I say, unzipping my lunch pail.

"What's wrong?"

"Oh, Lydia told Mrs. C. that I am the one who wrote the note Owen and Samir were throwing at each other."

"Did you?" Bray asks, looking shocked.

"Of course not, but what if Mrs. C. doesn't believe me?"

"Then you will just need to find out who did."

"Easy for you to say," I grumble. As I take out my sandwich a note falls on the table.

"Not another one," I complain.

How did Lydia get inside my lunch bag?

As I open the note, I breathe a sigh of relief.

"Oh, it's another clue from my dad."

"Read it, read it," Bray sings.

I laugh as I read, "I just want to dance; I just want to sing."

"Wait, what?" Bray asks, grabbing the paper from my hand.

"I just want to dance; I just want to sing?" she reads again. "What's that supposed to mean?"

"Obviously, I am going to dance with lizards," I say.

Bray laughs out loud. "Now I've gotta see that!"

CHAPTER FOUR

CLOSE CALL

I didn't see Mrs. Clemmons at lunch, so I asked one of the teacher's aides if I could go back to the classroom to look for her.

The aide looked at me funny, but finally said, "Okay, but if she isn't in the classroom, you come straight back."

I think all the staff have me on a secret watch list or something. Perhaps my poster is hung up in the teacher's lounge.

As I walk down the hallway, I notice that the light is off in the classroom. A normal student might turn around and go back to the lunch yard, but I am not a normal student. I am a super detective. Or at least, I will be one once I solve this case.

Maybe Mrs. Clemmons still has that note on her desk, and I can analyze the handwriting. I sneak into the classroom and see the crumpled note sitting in the trashcan. *Bingo!*

I open up the note carefully. The handwriting is very precise and neat. Not many fourth graders I know write like this. I smooth out the note on a desk and fold it into a small square. Just as I put the paper in my pocket, I hear a horrible noise.

I deep, growly sort of noise. I freeze in the dark classroom and turn around slowly.

Mrs. Clemmons is lying face down on her desk. Her hand is holding a half-eaten sandwich.

Oh no, someone poisoned Mrs. Clemmons!

I rush over to her and shake her shoulder.

"Mrs. Clemmons, are you alright? Can you hear me?"

She sits up in a panic and looks at me.

"Blondie?"

"Thank goodness, you are all right! Don't listen to Lydia, she didn't tell you the truth. You are my favorite teacher, and I would never hurt you."

Mrs. Clemmons starts chuckling and stands up to turn on the light.

"Slow down, Blondie. You are talking way too fast and not making any sense. Would you care to explain?"

"Okay," I say shyly. "It's just that Lydia told you I wrote that note. The one that said, 'Mrs. C is going to get it, and I promise I didn't.'"

"I never thought you did, Blondie," Mrs. Clemmons said reassuringly.

"Even after what Lydia said?"

"I know you wouldn't write something like that, but Lydia did say you were mad about your book report grade. Were you planning on talking to me about that?" she asks.

"Well, yes. I don't know. Maybe?" I answer, unsure what to say.

"I'm listening."

"It's just that you said not to use computers to design your covers, and then you gave Mark a better grade than me, even though he obviously used a computer."

"Hmm, did I really say that?" she asks, thoughtfully.

"You wrote it on the instruction sheet."

Mrs. Clemmons opens one of her file drawers and looks through the papers. She then pulls out of a pink paper and studies it carefully.

"You are right, Blondie. I forgot to change the rules from last year. I appreciate you following the rules, and I will change your grade based on your effort."

"Oh, thank you so much, Mrs. Clemmons," I squeal.

"But next time, just come talk to me instead of telling everyone you are mad."

"I…yes, Mrs. Clemmons," I say. I didn't think telling her that Lydia was just a nosey, no-good would help my situation.

"And Blondie," Mrs. Clemmons continues.

"Yes?"

"Why were you shaking me when you should be in the lunch yard?"

"Oh, that," I say, blushing slightly. "I came in here to talk to you about the note and thought someone poisoned your sandwich."

Mrs. Clemmons laughs.

"Oh, Blondie. You watch too many mystery movies."

It was no use arguing because she was definitely right. However, it was very odd that she was sleeping. Who falls asleep in the middle of eating a sandwich? Only someone that is eating a sandwich with something suspicious in it, and I am going to catch who is sneaking suspicious things into Mrs. Clemmons' sandwich and brownies.

CHAPTER FIVE

THE THREATENING NOTE

"How did you like the clue in your lunchbox yesterday, kiddo?" My dad asks as I sit down for breakfast.

"Um, it was great, dad," I answer.

He laughs.

"I take it you didn't solve the mystery yet?"

"Oh, I am pretty close," I fib. I don't want him to doubt my detective abilities.

"Sure you are, sweetheart," my dad smiles, coyly. "Here's your next clue." He hands me a folded piece of paper.

I open the piece of paper and read:

My full name is Elizabeth, but that is not what I'm known by.

"Pretty clever, huh?" my dad laughs again. He was having way too much fun with this.

"Any guesses to what the clue means?"

"That my Aunt Beth is coming over this weekend?" I guess.

"So close," my dad shouts. "But no."

"Did you get another clue today," Bray asks as I enter the school's courtyard.

"Yeah, but don't get too excited. It still doesn't mean anything to me," I say and hand her the paper.

"My full name is Elizabeth, but that is not what I'm known by?" Bray reads out loud.

"So obviously we are looking for someone named Elizabeth but everyone calls her something different," Bray says, excitedly.

"That's what I thought, but the only person I know is my Aunt Beth, and my dad said she wasn't coming over this weekend."

"Back up, what exactly did you guess?"

"That my Aunt Beth was coming over this weekend."

"And what did your dad say to that."

"So close, but no," I answer.

"So maybe it is your Aunt Beth, but maybe she's not coming to you."

I bite the inside of my cheek as I think.

"Where does your aunt live?" Bray asks.

"Texas."

"Oh my goodness! The Texas horned lizard is the state reptile of Texas," Bray shouts excitedly.

"How in the world did you know that?" I ask.

"My older sister had to do her state report on Texas last year. She made me listen to her presentation like a gazillion times," Bray says.

"Okay, but what does that have to do with anything?"

"The lizard clue, silly," Bray says. "Do you still have that clue?"

I nod and pull it out of my backpack.

"Rock, paper, scissors, chameleons, toads, and lizards," I read to her.

"See, the clue was about lizards, and your Aunt Beth lives in the state that has a lot of lizards, what else could it be?" she asks.

"But what about the clue from yesterday," I ask, opening that paper up. "I just want to dance; I just want to sing," I read.

"That sounds so familiar, but I can't put my finger on it," Bray says. "Maybe your dad just meant that you are going to have fun at your Aunt Beth's house?"

"I don't know. I'll ask him tonight when I get home."

"Make sure you call me right away to tell me if I was right," Bray says.

"Okay," I laugh.

"You aren't the only amazing detective around here, you know," Bray says, jokingly.

"I still have my suspicions," I answer.

The bell rings and the school doors open. As I enter the fourth-grade room, I notice that Mrs. Clemmons is not here again. Before this week, Mrs. Clemmons has always been waiting for us in the classroom, usually with the journaling prompt on the board.

I decide to take the long way to my seat and walk past Mrs. Clemmons desk slowly to see if there are any new clues. I see a yellow sticky note with bold cursive saying:

I know your secret. If you don't tell the others by Friday. I will. –A

"Bray," I whisper, trying not to attract anyone else's attention, but she doesn't hear me.

"Bray," I say a little louder, but by the time she turns around, Mrs. Clemmons is entering the classroom.

"Good morning, class," Mrs. Clemmons says cheerfully. I sneak away to my desk, hoping she doesn't notice that I was looking at her papers.

I watch her set her bag down and sit at her desk. Her brows furrow as she reads the note, and she quickly rips the note in half and throws it in the trashcan.

I grab my notebook and write as fast as I can.

"Blondie, I haven't assigned the writing prompt yet," Mrs. Clemmons laughs.

The whole class looks at me, and I embarrassingly close my detective notebook and slide it back into my backpack.

"Speaking of writing prompt, here is today's prompt," she says as she walks toward the chalkboard.

Is it ever a good idea to keep a secret from your friends and family? Why or why not?

My eyes felt like they were going to pop out of my eye sockets. Mrs. Clemmons was in serious trouble and she was asking us for advice!

I scribbled down my answer as quick as I could and raise my hand.

"Yes, Blondie," Mrs. Clemmons says.

"Are we going to take turns reading our answers today?" I ask.

"Probably not. We usually only read our answers on Friday's prompt."

"Are you sure you don't want to hear our answers for today?" I ask again.

Mrs. Clemmons laughs. "You must really want to read what you wrote, don't you, Blondie?"

"I just think it could save someone's life if they were in a bad situation."

"Well, by all means. Class, let's listen to Blondie's answer."

Everyone turns to look at me, and I can feel a lump develop in my throat. I swallow and begin reading, "No secret is worth keeping if it could get you in trouble or could put you in danger. If you are in doubt, always tell a trusted adult or the police."

"Is that all?" Mrs. Clemmons asks.

I nod.

"That is a very good answer, Blondie, but remember, you need to make your prompts at least one page long, single-spaced."

It's like she wasn't even listening to me!

I nod again and continue to write. This time with less urgency. Mrs. Clemmons might not take my advice, but that doesn't mean I am going to give up on her case.

CHAPTER SIX

MYSTERIOUS A

I sneak my detective notebook into my lunch pail and bring it with me when the lunch bell rings.

"We've got some serious work to do," I tell Bray as she sits down with her tray.

"Work? What are you talking about? I already solved your dad's case."

"I'm talking about Mrs. Clemmons' case."

"What case?"

"Someone is trying to hurt or embarrass Mrs. Clemmons," I say quietly.

"Why would someone want to do that?" she asks.

"I don't know, but all of the evidence is here."

I open up my detective notebook and show her what I've been working on.

"Let's take a look at all of the clues. First, she came to school sweaty and pale, like someone was chasing her. Then she wrote, 'What would you do if someone was chasing you?' on the board."

"She was probably just running to class because she was late," Bray interrupted.

"That's another thing. She has been late twice this week. Mrs. Clemmons is never late."

"I'm still not convinced," says Bray.

"Then what about this?" I ask, holding up my brownie bag.

"Eww, what is that?" she asks, poking at a moldy spot that has grown on the brownie.

I pull the bag quickly away from her so she can't ruin my evidence.

"Remember the plate of brownies?"

Bray nods.

"Remember how she got sick afterward?"

"Oh yeah," Bray says. "But how can we prove it was the brownies?"

"Because she got sick right after eating them, and after I get this brownie tested, I will know for sure what is in them."

"How are you going to get them tested?"

"I'm still trying to figure it out, but I just know that they are poisoned?"

"How could you possibly know that?" Bray asks.

"Why else would someone leave brownies without leaving a note. If you gave Mrs. Clemmons brownies, wouldn't you leave a note?"

"Of course, I would want her to know I gave them to her," Bray answers.

"Exactly! The person who gave her these brownies didn't want her to know who gave them to her. They didn't want to be blamed for poisoning Mrs. Clemmons."

Bray makes an "eh" type of sound but doesn't say anything else.

"Also, what about these two notes." I pull out the crumpled note that Owen and Samir were throwing at each other, as well as the ripped note that Mrs. Clemmons threw away that morning.

"Where did you get these from?" Bray asks, picking up one of the notes.

"The trash."

"Um, eww," Bray says, putting down the note in disgust.

"Did you read them?" I ask, ignoring her comment.

She takes a moment to read both notes.

"Who would write that?" she asks.

"That's what I am trying to figure out."

"Well, they are obviously written by two different people," Bray points out. "Look the g's on each note are written differently."

"Great work, Watson," I shout. "I mean, Bray."

We both laugh and look at the notes again.

"So who's name starts with an A?"

"Alex?" Bray asks.

"Alex's writing looks like a kindergartner's scribbles," I answer.

"True. The note is written with really good handwriting like a teacher would do."

"Maybe it is from a teacher?" I add.

"But I thought all of the teachers liked each other," Bray says.

"What if Mrs. Clemmons found out something she shouldn't have?"

"Like what?" Bray asks.

"I don't. Maybe she did something to make the other teachers mad."

"Let's not get ahead of ourselves," Bray reminds me. "Let's just focus on who A is."

"Well, there is Mr. Riley, Mrs. Johnson, Miss Skinner, Mrs. Lennard, and Mr. Morgan. None of those start with an A."

"What if they used their first name?" Bray asks.

"But we don't know the teachers' first names."

We sit in silence, both thinking.

"I think their names are all listed in the yearbook," I say.

"Brilliant. Only one problem," Bray says.

"What's that?" I ask.

"How do we get our hands on a yearbook?"

"I have one at home," I say.

"That means we have to wait until after school," she sighs.

"I know, but that's all we can do for now. Until then, just keep your eyes out for clues."

"Like what kind of clues?" Bray asks.

"Anything that looks suspicious, weird behavior, mysterious notes, items that don't belong."

Bray nods.

CHAPTER SEVEN

COMPROMISED EVIDENCE

I practically trip over George and Emma, my two dachshunds, as I run up to my room after school. I have been anxiously waiting to get home so that I can crack open last year's yearbook.

George licks me excitedly.

"Not now," I say, pushing my backpack in between me and him as a barrier.

George pushes the backpack furiously with his nose. It is very distracting. While he did help me solve the case with Samir's lunch box last month, I definitely did not want his big, wet nose in my face right now.

"George," I exclaim. "Can't you see I have very important detective work to do?"

I throw the backpack towards my bed, and he follows it.

I turn all my attention to my bookcase. I spot my third-grade yearbook and pull it off the shelf. I flip as quickly as I can to the faculty page.

"Mr. Terry Riley, fifth grade," I begin reading out loud. "Nope."

"Not Mrs. Clemmons," I say, looking past her name.

"Mrs. Mary Johnson, third grade. No. Miss Linda Skinner, second grade. No. Mrs. Susan Lennard, first grade. No again. And Mr. Robert Morgan. Another big, fat no." I throw my yearbook down, frustrated.

If it's not a student and not a teacher, then who wrote the note?

Just then I hear the phone ring.

"Blondie," my mom calls. I run down the stairs.

"It's Bray."

"Oh yay!" I say.

"Are you done with your homework?" my mom asks, sternly.

"No, but I promise I won't talk long," I say.

"Okay," she says as she hands me the phone. "Ten minutes' tops."

I nod and run back up the stairs.

"There are no teachers that start with A," Bray says as I put the phone to my ear.

"I know. I just saw. So who else could it be?"

"Maybe see if any of last year's fourth graders held a grudge against Mrs. Clemmons?" Bray asks, unsure.

"That's a great idea. Do you have your yearbook in front of you?" I ask.

"Yep," she answers.

I close the door to my room and sit down in front of the yearbook.

"Great. Me too."

"Oh, look, there was an Allison Moore in Mrs. Clemmons class last year," Bray points out.

"I don't think she still goes to our school," I say. I talked to almost all of the fifth graders when I was trying to solve Owen's food fight mystery, and I couldn't recall talking to an Allison.

"How about Allegra Price?" I ask.

"Definitely not her," Bray says.

"Why not?"

"I sometimes carpool with her. She's way too nice," Bray answers.

"Well, sometimes the nicest people can surprise you," I say.

"I just don't think she would ever do something mean to anyone, especially a teacher."

"Okay, but let's not cross her off the suspect list quite yet," I say.

"Hold on a second," I exclaim.

I turned back to the faculty page.

"We looked at all of the teachers, but we didn't look at the teacher's aides," I say.

"You're right," Bray exclaims. I can hear her flipping pages in her yearbook.

"Miss Amy Stella," we shout together.

"But what would she have against Mrs. Clemmons," Bray asks.

"I don't know. Wait a second. Remember how Mrs. Clemmons got mad at her last week for being on her phone during her recess duty?"

"She didn't seem that mad," Bray says.

"Well, that was just what we saw. What if Mrs. Clemmons yelled at her or told Principal Johnson?"

"You're right!" Bray says excitedly. "We have to talk to her tomorrow during recess."

"Argh!" I scream as I look over at my backpack.

"Blondie, what is it? What happened?" Bray shouts concerned in the phone.

"It's just George. He's eaten the brownie that was supposed to be evidence."

"But you said it could be poisoned."

My eye opened wide. Initially, I was just annoyed that George had eaten a crucial piece of evidence, but Bray was right. If the brownie was poisonous, then George could be in serious trouble.

"I'll see you tomorrow," I say concerned.

I hang up before Bray can say anything else and pick up George. For a dachshund puppy, he is quite heavy. I have to use the stair railing to balance myself while I carry him downstairs. He doesn't help me with all of his wriggling and squirming.

"Mom," I shout, worried.

My mom looks up from her spot on the couch, where she was balancing her laptop on one leg and a legal pad on the other.

"Yes, sweetheart."

"George is in trouble. We need to take him to the pet hospital immediately."

"Slow down, Blondie," my mom says as she puts her hand up. "Start from the beginning."

"There's no time, mom. Can't you see that George is going to die?"

My mom looks at George, who is wiggling excitedly in my arms.

"He looks perfectly fine to me, love."

"But he just ate a brownie, which might or might not have been poisonous."

At that moment George starts whining loudly.

"See, he is in a lot of pain," I say.

My mom just laughs. "Oh sweetheart. He is whining because Emma is playing with his toy. Put him down, and you will see."

Determined to prove her wrong, I set him down. I was expecting him to roll over in agonizing pain, but instead he runs happily over to Emma and leaps on her back.

"Well maybe the poison hasn't had time to affect him yet."

"Why do you think the brownie was poisonous, because it was chocolate and chocolate is poisonous to dogs?"

How do you explain to your mom that you suspect that someone is trying to hurt your favorite teacher? I knew she wouldn't understand if I tried.

"Yes," I agree. "Chocolate is very dangerous for dogs."

My mom looks down at her computer and begins typing.

"Well, one vet wrote an article saying that as long as the dog is not showing any signs of discomfort, they probably didn't consume enough chocolate to be dangerous."

"But mom," I say.

She holds up her finger. "But, she also suggests feeding the dog a runny egg and taking them on a long walk just to be sure."

I try to force a smile as my mom walks into the kitchen and grabs a pan.

"Go ahead and get George and Emma's leashes," my mom says.

I grab their leashes and clip them to their collars. Emma sits patiently as I clip her pink, sparkly leash on. "Good girl," I say, giving her a pet.

George, on the other hand, is a complete spaz. Every time I get close to George he dashes in the opposite direction. He is so excited to go for a walk that he can't sit still.

Finally, my mom puts a plate of runny eggs on the floor, which gives me 5.5 seconds to clip on his leash as he swallows the eggs without chewing.

"How long am I supposed to walk them for?" I ask.

My mom laughs and answers, "Oh, you will know."

I'm not sure what that means, but the dogs pull me towards the front door before I can ask any more questions.

"Okay, okay, calm down," I try to shout over their happy yaps. I open the door, and they continue to drag me along. For small dogs, they sure do have a lot of power.

As Emma and George sniff every tree that lines the sidewalk, I can't help but think about who could have left those brownies on Mrs. Clemmons' desk, and who would want to hurt her.

Even if it was Miss Stella, it still didn't explain who wrote the note, "Mrs. C is going to get it." Maybe Miss Stella wasn't working alone? Was she working with another teacher or teacher's aide?

A lightbulb goes off in my head. A picture flashes in my mind of last year's fourth-grade class. I remember reading, "Julie Stella," under one of the girl's pictures. I remember now. Miss Stella said that she had a niece in Mr. Riley's class that year. What if they are working together? What if Julie didn't like Mrs. Clemmons as much as I did?

I look down at the dogs. I wonder when I can take them home. I have some important detective work to do now that I have a lead on the top two suspects. The dogs dart back and forth across the sidewalk, smelling anything they can find.

"Hey Blondie," a voice calls.

I look up in surprise.

"Oh, hey, Owen."

I wasn't paying attention to where the dogs were going and didn't realize we were already at Owen's house. Owen was kind of a pain at school, but as a neighbor, he wasn't too bad.

George wriggled furiously when he saw Owen. After a few hard jerks, he was able to squeeze his chubby neck free from the collar and leash. He runs up to Owen quicker than he ran to the plate of runny eggs my mom served him minutes earlier.

Owen bends down with a smile, and George covers him in slobbery kisses.

"Since you're not doing anything, Owen, I was wondering if I can ask you a few questions."

Owen looked up, still holding George's head in his hands. "Oh no, what do you think I did now?"

"Nothing," I laugh. "I was just wondering if you noticed anything strange with Mrs. Clemmons."

"What do you mean?" Owen asks.

"Like has Mrs. Clemmons seemed to be in danger or just acting odder than usual?"

Owen thought quietly for a moment while he scratched behind George's ears.

"Now that you mention it," he starts.

"Yes," I say excitedly.

"Nah, it's probably nothing."

"Just tell me," I demand.

"Okay, okay, relax," he says standing up. "It's just on Tuesday I fell when playing basketball. I cut my leg. It wasn't that bad, just pretty bloody." He lifts up his pant leg to show me a large scab.

"I'm sorry to hear that," I say, trying to sound sympathetic. Detective lesson 43: Always be nice to witnesses even when they tell you irrelevant information.

"But what does that have to do with Mrs. Clemmons?" I ask.

"Oh, well I went in the class to ask for a bandage, and she ran me to the office and asked the secretary to take care of it. Then she ran out of the office with her hand over her mouth. I'm pretty sure I heard her say, 'I'm going to be sick.'"

"Interesting. Very interesting," I say. "Did you notice her eating anything before she took you to the office."

"Um, I don't think so. Eww! Gross!" Owen shouted with wide eyes. He was no longer looking at me, but instead behind me.

I turned around quickly to see George squatting on Owen's driveway. Let's just say that the runny eggs were now a runny something else.

So that's what my mom had meant when she said that I will know when the walk is over.

"Oops, sorry about that," I say, trying not to laugh.

"Aren't you going to clean it up?" he asks.

"With what? I didn't bring anything."

"Don't you know that you are always supposed to bring a plastic bag when you take your dogs for a walk?" Owen looks beyond disgusted, which is a shock coming from someone who flicks his boogers across the classroom.

"I'll keep that in mind," I say, bending down to squeeze George's collar over his head again.

"See ya tomorrow, Owen," I wave, walking away.

"Yeah, yeah," he says, grabbing the hose from the bushes.

CHAPTER EIGHT

Squary at Cookie?

It's Thursday, and I am not closer to solving who is messing with Mrs. Clemmons. Owens story definitely had me convinced that something strange was going on, but I still only had one suspect – Miss Stella, who might or not be accompanied by her niece.

I share my suspicions with Bray before school starts.

"It seems like a long shot, but it can't hurt to ask them a few questions," Bray says.

The school bell rings, and I tell Bray to keep her eyes open for any clues when we walk in.

She nods and proceeds to look around the fourth-grade classroom very obviously.

I will have to show her how to look for clues more discreetly after we solve this case.

I look for clues too as I walk towards my seat. There are no notes, food, or other suspicious things on Mrs. Clemmons' desk.

Mrs. Clemmons looks happier than usual as she writes the journal prompt on the board. "Where would be your dream vacation if you had all the money in the world?" she wrote on the board.

No mysterious notes or writing prompts. Maybe Mrs. Clemmons is no longer in trouble.

"Before I forget," Mrs. Clemmons says, reaching her hand into her pocket. "This note was on my desk, Blondie. You can go after you finish your journaling."

Mrs. Clemmons drops the note on the ground before she hands it to me. As she bends down to pick it up, two buttons on her blouse pop off. One falls to the floor and the other shoots across the room.

The classroom fills with roars of laughter, but I noticed that Bray looks directly at me. It is like I know what she is thinking. Was that an accident or did someone do that to Mrs. Clemmons shirt on purpose? It's not like Mrs. Clemmons was a big woman. In fact, she was quite small, and if I remember correctly, she was always bending over picking things off the ground. Yet this was the first time that one of her buttons popped off.

Mrs. Clemmons cheeks flush a rosy-pink color as she looks down at her button-down shirt.

"Oh, dear," she says. "Well, that's embarrassing. Class, I am going to change my shirt really quick. I know that was very funny, but try to settle down and finish your journaling prompts."

Mrs. Clemmons digs through her teacher bag and pulls out an extra shirt. *What is up with teachers keeping extra clothes with them at all times?*

"Blondie, can you stand in the front of the room and write down names of people who talk while I am gone?"

I nod and walk towards the front of the room.

As she leaves the room, I see a few kids whispering and then quickly stop when they see me glaring at them.

I look out the door to make sure Mrs. Clemmons is out of earshot.

"Alright, fourth graders," I say. "I know someone did that to Mrs. Clemmons shirt, and I know someone is trying to make her sick."

Some kids in the back of the class whisper to each other, but I can't hear what they are saying.

"My point is that if it is you, I will find out, and you will be in trouble. It is best to come clean now."

Before I can get anyone to confess, Owen hisses loudly, "She's coming!"

Everyone quickly grabs their journals and pencils and start writing.

"Very impressive, class," Mrs. Clemmons says as she enters the room again.

"Thank you, Blondie. You can sit down now," she says waving her hand towards me. "Oh and here is that note," she adds, handing me the note that caused the whole shirt debacle.

Blondelle McGhee: Come to the office.

I studied the note carefully. The writing looked oddly familiar. When I got to my desk, I pulled out the crumpled note.

Mrs. C is going to get it.

Same slant, same dot over the "i", and same curvature in the "C". Could it be?

I quickly wrote about my dream vacation in my journal, although half of my thoughts were on the two notes. As soon as I finished, I shut my journal quickly and folded both notes in my hand.

Mrs. Brown, the secretary smiles at me as I walk into the office.

"Hello, Blondie. Your mom stopped by to drop off your lunch," she says, handing me the brown paper bag.

"Also, she said your grandma was going to pick you up after school, so be sure to look for her car during pick up time."

I nod.

"Mrs. Brown, can I ask you something?" I ask cautiously.

"Sure, dear."

I spread out the crumbled note on her desk.

"Did you write this?"

"Mrs. C is going to get it," she reads carefully. "Well, it sure looks like my writing, but I can't remember writing it. Where did you get it from?"

"I found it on the floor in Mrs. Clemmons' class," I say. I didn't want to get in trouble.

She rubs her chin gently and repeats, "Mrs. C is going to get it...Oh, I remember now. That was a note I left for Principal Johnson saying that Mrs. Clemmons was going to get something from one of the parents."

"Get what?" I ask.

"Oh, that is nothing for you to worry about. It was just some information we needed on someone."

"So you aren't mad at Mrs. Clemmons or want to hurt her?"

Mrs. Brown makes a loud squawking noise. "What?! Of course not," she laughs. "The other teachers were right about your wild imagination, Blondie."

I try not to look offended.

"I'm innocent today," Mrs. Brown says, giggling with her hands up. "You can go back to class now, Blondie."

As I walk back to the classroom, I peer into my lunch bag. I spot what I was looking for – a clue. I might not be able to solve Mrs. Clemmons case before lunch, but maybe I can solve what my dad is trying to say.

What in the world is this? I am completely thrown off by today's clue. Maybe each picture means something.

Fly, square, plus E, at cookie?

I hide my clue in my pocket until I get back to my desk.

Fly squary at cookie? I try again. *No, that doesn't make sense.*

I cover up all the pictures with another piece of paper. Maybe if I look at each picture separately I will solve it.

Now that I look at the fly, I notice that he has stripes. *Flies don't have stripes. Oh, it's a bee!*

Be squary at cookie? I say in my mind again. *It still doesn't make sense.*

Squary? What is a squary and why is it red? It would have been helpful if dad made the bee yellow, then I would have known it was a bee. *Oh, it's not squary!* Dad, wanted me to say 'red' and then plus the e would be 'ready". Be ready at...ugh, it still looks like a cookie no matter how I turn the paper.

I look at the board. Mrs. Clemmons was teaching how to solve a new math problem.

"When you see part of the problem in parentheses, you want to solve that part first."

She writes:

2 x (1+4)-2=

"So when you see a problem with parentheses, you are going to act like the parentheses is its own little bubble that needs to be popped before moving on to the rest of the problem," she says while drawing a circle to the side of the board.

"What's one plus four class?" she asks.

"Five," the class answers together.

"Good," she says drawing five lines inside the circle. "Now that you solved the parentheses, you need to solve any multiplication or division before you solve any addition or subtraction outside of this bubble." She points to the circle with five lines inside.

"I've got it," I exclaim excitedly.

"You know the answer?" Mrs. Clemmons asks with a big smile.

"Oh, um. No. Sorry. I got excited about something else."

"Try to keep your attention and excitement on the math lesson, Blondie."

I nod.

"Like I was saying," Mrs. Clemmons continues. You are going to multiply before you subtract, so..."

I drown out her voice and look down at my clue again. *It isn't a cookie. I need to count the dots in the circle. One, two, three, four, five, six.*

Be ready at six.

Finally, I solved one of dad's clues.

CHAPTER NINE

QUESTIONING SUSPECT A

"Should we talk to Julie or Miss Stella first?" Bray asks me as we walk to the playground for recess.

"Let's start with Julie if we can find her," I say.

"Should we ask a fifth grader where she usually hangs out at recess?" she asks.

"We can try. Sometimes fifth graders are mean." I scan the playground to look for the nearest fifth grader.

"There's one," I say, pointing at a tall girl by the basketball hoop.

"Hi, do you know who Julie Stella usually hangs out with at recess," I ask the girl.

"Julie didn't come to school today. Why?" she says dribbling a basketball.

"Oh, no reason. Was she here yesterday?" I ask, hoping I can find out more.

"She's been gone all week. She was sick and had to get her tonsils out, or something like that." She shoots the ball in the air and it goes through the net effortlessly.

"Do you know if she ever was mad at Mrs. Clemmons or anything like that?"

The tall girl stops dribbling the ball and looks at me funny.

"Everyone loves Mrs. Clemmons. Why are you asking so many weird questions?"

"Just curious," I say.

"Okay, well, I'm going to working on my free throws now," she says.

"Go ahead," I say, watching her.

"Preferably alone," she says.

"Right. Thank you for your help."

"What now?" Bray asks as we walk away.

"Well, if Julie has been gone all week, then she is no longer a suspect. Which makes me have my doubts about Miss Stella." I explain.

"But there is no other teacher or teacher's aide with a name that starts with A," Bray says.

"Well, I guess it can't hurt to ask her if she recognizes the note," I agree.

We spot Miss Stella standing next to the fence, playing with her whistle necklace.

"Hi Miss Stella," I say as we walk up to her.

"Hi girls. Why aren't you playing?"

"Well, we, I mean I was wondering something," I say, hesitantly.

"Yes?"

I pulled out the ripped note from my pocket and hold it in front of her.

"Is this your handwriting?"

She squints down and looks at the note.

"Yes, it is. How did you know?" she laughs.

"You are the only adult at Graham Elementary whose name starts with an A," I explain.

"You caught me," she laughs again.

"Well, what does the note mean?"

"I'm afraid it is none of your business. Now why don't you girls go swing. There's only ten minutes left of recess."

"How come you are trying to hurt Mrs. Clemmons? Are you the one that left the poisonous brownies and ruined her shirt too?"

"What?!" Miss Stella exclaims. "I have no idea what you are talking about."

"Then tell us what the note means," I demand.

"We will have a talk with Mrs. Clemmons after recess, but I think it is a good idea for you girls to go play instead of talking to me rudely. I don't want to send you to the principal's office for disrespect."

"Come on," Bray urges, tugging on my arm.

"Alright," I say, allowing Bray to drag me away from Miss Stella.

Once Miss Stella is out of ear shot, I turn to Bray, "Why did you drag me away?"

"You heard the lady. She was going to send us to the principal's office."

"I was just about to get her to crack," I say.

"I don't think so. I just really don't want us to get into trouble."

Before we can reach the swing set, the bell rings, signaling that recess is over.

"Uh oh," I whisper to Bray as we were walking to get in line with the rest of our class.

"What?" I ask cautiously.

"Miss Stella is looking at us. Do you think she is going to get us in trouble with Mrs. Clemmons?"

I try to look unsuspiciously at Miss Stella, but it is hard to see her now that all the classes are lining up.

"We can't get in trouble," I explain. "We haven't done anything wrong. She is the one that left a mysterious note on Mrs. C's desk."

"I sure hope you are right," Bray says nervously. "I really don't want to get in trouble."

Sure enough, the moment Bray and I sat in our seats, Miss Stella was whispering something to Mrs. Clemmons by her desk. Mrs. Clemmons brows furrowed as she looked over at me, and she nodded a few times as Miss Stella told her something.

"I told you," Bray mouths to me across the room. She twists her hands together nervously.

"Don't worry," I try to mouth back.

"Class," Mrs. Clemmons says. "Time to get out your social studies books."

Bray looks relieved.

"See," I mouth and give her a thumbs up.

I knew Mrs. C would take our side. Maybe she has known all this time what Miss Stella has been up to.

"Blondie and Bray, please follow me."

Brays eyes bulge, as she stands up to go to Mrs. Clemmons' desk. I have to admit that I am slightly nervous too. *Would Mrs. C believe our side of the story?*

CHAPTER TEN

MISUNDERSTANDING

As Bray and I walk out of the classroom, we see Miss Stella leaning against the wall with her arms folded.

"Would you girls like to explain why you talked disrespectfully to Miss Stella at recess?" Mrs. Clemmons asks.

Bray shoves her hands in her pockets and looks at me.

So much for being my Watson, I thought.

"It's all my fault," I tell Mrs. Clemmons. "Bray didn't have anything to do with it."

"Thank you for saying that Blondie, but you still haven't answered my question."

Looks like I won't be solving my case after all. Time to lay it all on the table.

"Well, you see, I just wanted to know if Miss Stella wrote you this note," I say, fishing the ripped note out of my pocket.

Mrs. Clemmons reads the note.

"Which I told you I did, Blondie, but then you accused me of poisoning Mrs. Clemmons." Miss Stella adds.

Oh right, that.

"Is that true, Blondie?" Mrs. Clemmons asks.

I look down at my shoe and make circles on the ground with my toe.

"Well, yes, but it is only because I wanted to catch who was trying to hurt you."

"Hurt me?" Mrs. Clemmons asks.

"Yes, there are a lot of strange things going on, and I think someone is trying to get back at you Mrs. Clemmons."

"Why would you say that?"

"For one, you were late twice this week," I say.

"I am human, Blondie," Mrs. Clemmons laughs.

"Two, the mysterious journaling prompts," I add.

"Those come out of my lesson book, so I am not sure how mysterious they could be."

"Well, what about getting sick after the brownies and seeing Owen's bloody cut?"

Mrs. Clemmons smile disappears.

"And your shirt buttons fell off, and you fell asleep while eating your sandwich. Who does that unless they are poisoned?" I continue.

Miss Stella laughs loudly, and Mrs. Clemmons shoots her a stern look.

"See, I'm right. Someone is messing with you, aren't they?"

"Someone is messing with her all right," Miss Stella laughs.

"Amy, you aren't helping the matter," Mrs. Clemmons says, not smiling.

"Just tell everyone already. What's the big deal?" Miss Stella says.

Mrs. Clemmons closes her eyes and rubs the bridge of her nose.

"You are right. Girls, get back in your seats." Mrs. Clemmons says.

Did I miss something here? Did they know about the case all along?

Bray breathes a sigh of relief, and we both go back to our desks. Of course, every fourth grader looks at us curiously.

"All right, class." Mrs. Clemmons says loudly as she walks back in. I'm pretty sure I saw Owen jump from fright.

"I have something important to tell you."

Is she going to tell us that she is in trouble and has to flee the country? Or maybe she has been a secret spy this whole time and being a teacher is her undercover persona?

"Some of you have noticed that I have been late a few times this week and have gotten sick from weird things, like brownies or cuts," her eyes dart towards Owen, who blushes and looks down.

"Well, I have been acting and feeling weird because Mr. Clemmons and I are going to have a baby?"

Gasps fill the air, and Mrs. Clemmons holds her hand up to quiet everyone.

"Don't worry. The doctor said I should start to feel better soon," she adds.

"But who is going to be our teacher?" Mark shouts out.

"Me, of course. The baby isn't due until summer break."

I raise my hand.

"Yes, Blondie."

"But Miss Stella said that someone is messing with you, so what does a baby have to do with any of that?"

Mrs. Clemmons laughs. "Oh, Blondie. She was only joking. She meant that the baby was making it hard for me to be normal. Sometimes when you are pregnant, foods that you love make you sick, you fall asleep randomly, and you forget things."

I think back on all of the clues I wrote down in my detective notebook. It all makes sense now.

Another fourth grader, Georgia raises her hand. "Is it a boy or a girl?"

"That is still a mystery to me, though I'm sure Blondie could figure it out for me," she laughs.

"Will you name the baby after me?" Owen asks.

"We will see," Mrs. Clemmons laughs. "But for now, let's focus on social studies. We will have plenty of time to talk about the new baby."

CHAPTER ELEVEN

CRACKING DAD'S CLUES

"You'll never guess what Mrs. Clemmons told us today," I say excitedly when my family sits down for dinner.

"Hmm, let me guess," my dad says, closing his eyes, putting his fingers to his temple.

"You are never going to guess," I say.

"I think I'm getting something," my dad says. "Is that a picture of a baby I see? Yes! Mrs. Clemmons is having a baby."

My mouth dropped open. "How did you know that?"

"I read your mind with my amazing mind reading abilities," my dad proclaims.

"And your teacher emailed all of the parents before you got home," my mom laughs.

"No fair," I pout.

"Sorry, Blondie. I should have let you tell me the exciting news," my dad adds. "Do you have any news about my clues, though?"

"I thought you could read minds," I laugh.

"Oh, right, yes," he says, tapping his fingers on his temples again. "It is looking a bit hazy in that mind of yours."

I laugh again. "I'm still working on it. I have been a little busy trying to figure out what was wrong with Mrs. Clemmons."

"You suspected she was pregnant?" my mom asks.

"No, I thought someone was trying to hurt her. She kept getting sick and even fell asleep in the middle of eating a sandwich."

My mom laughs. "I remember those days."

"What do you mean?" I ask.

"Once when I was pregnant with you, I cried for two hours because I thought I lost Jana. It turned out that I had asked Grammie to come over and take her to school that morning."

"And don't get me started on that number of pickles your mom ate every day," my dad adds. My mom playfully hits him on the shoulder.

"Well, there is only one more clue. I really hope you can figure out this mystery before Saturday," my dad says.

"What happens if I don't?" I ask.

"Great and horrible things," my dad says dramatically.

"Here's your last clue, sweetheart. Use it wisely," my dad says Friday morning as he drops me off for school.

"Isn't this your work badge? Don't you need it for work?" I ask.

"It's just a copy," he winks. "Have a great day at school."

I study his badge carefully. *John McGhee, Director of Security*. Underneath his name and job title is the Epic Center logo. The Epic Center is the place that all of the big basketball games and concerts take place.

I try to find a hidden message in the words and on his picture. *Is this a trick?*

"Blondie," Bray says, panting. "Didn't you hear me call your name?"

"No! I'm sorry. I'm trying to figure out this dumb clue," I say and hand her my dad's badge.

"Your dad's work badge?" she laughs. "What clue could possibly be hidden on it?"

"That's exactly what I was thinking."

"I just want to dance; I just want to sing, and if I believe than I can do anything," a voice sings out.

Bray stops walking.

"Did you hear that?" she asks.

"Hear what?" I ask.

"Someone was singing something," she says.

"Oh you mean that person singing the newest Lizzy Lizard song?" I say nonchalantly.

"Yes!" she shouts.

I look at her slightly confused.

"And?" I ask.

"Your clue!"

The lightbulb goes on in my head.

"Of course! How could I have been so silly?" I kneel down and take all of the clues out of my backpack.

"The lizard clue must be referring to Lizzy's last name," I say.

"And the Elizabeth clue means her first name," Bray adds, excitedly.

"And that clue with her song lyric verifies that it is her," I say. "And I got another clue telling me to be ready at six."

"So what do you think your dad's work badge means?" Bray asks.

"Do you think there is a concert this weekend?" I ask, my eyes wide with excitement.

"Oh my goodness, you are going to see Lizzy Lizard in person!" Bray shrieks.

"There is only one way to verify it. We need a newspaper with the weekly events."

"Do you think the office gets the newspaper?" Bray asks.

"Only one way to find out. It just seems too good to be true."

It is hard to walk to the office when I feel like skipping and jumping. Imagine me going to see Lizzy Lizard. The logical side of me kicks in. *Don't get too excited until you know all the facts, Blondie.*

"Good morning, girls, is there something I can help you with?" Mrs. Brown greets us.

"You don't happen to have a newspaper, do you?"

"A newspaper? I'm sorry I don't."

"Oh, thanks anyways," I say, hanging my head down.

"I guess you will just have to wait until you get home," Bray says quietly.

Finally, school is over! Now I can find a newspaper and confirm the clues. Even though I am 99% sure that I have cracked the case, it would be silly of me to just guess and not confirm my findings. In the real detective world, you can't just guess who the bad guy is and hope you are right.

The Friday school day went by so slowly, especially since I didn't have Mrs. Clemmons' case to think about. I still chuckle to myself thinking about all of the details. I should have known that no one would ever hurt Mrs. Clemmons.

"Mom, do we have a newspaper?" I ask, as she pulls into our driveway.

"No, but I think Mrs. Moore has one. You can take her some of the oatmeal cookies I baked yesterday."

I couldn't help but grimace. Mrs. Moore was our neighbor, and though she was really nice, her house was full of smelly cats and she tells very long stories.

"Can you go ask her?" I ask hopefully.

My mom laughs. "Nope. Go grab the plate of cookies from the table and head over. The sooner you go, the sooner you get your newspaper."

"If I am not back in ten minutes, it means I am being forced to listen to Mrs. Moore's opera collection against my will. Send reinforcements."

My mom laughs again. "Oh, Blondie."

I run in the house, throw my backpack down and grab the plate of cookies.

Whining fills the air. *I've been spotted!*

"George, I'll be right back."

George whines louder.

"Don't look at me like that. Last time I took you to Mrs. Moore's house you tried to eat Mr. Fluffy Tail."

George know starts to yap in between whines.

"I know, I know, you were just trying to play, but Mrs. Moore didn't see it that way."

His whining continues. *Will this dog stop at nothing?*

I throw an oatmeal cookie across the room, and he happily chases after it. "Don't tell anyone I gave you that," I say.

"Wish me luck, mom," I say as I pass her outside the door. "I may never be the same."

My mom just shakes her head and laughs.

I knock at the door.

No answer.

I knock again a bit louder.

Still no answer. Mrs. Moore always answers by the second knock, and she never goes anywhere. *Did something happen to Mrs. Moore?*

The door swings open, and Mrs. Moore appears with an eye mask on her forehead.

"Sorry I didn't hear you darling. I was just taking a short nap."

"I didn't mean to wake you Mrs. Moore. I just wanted to ask to borrow your newspaper."

"Oh, don't be silly. I love when you come to visit me. Come in, come in." She pulls me in and leads me to the couch.

"I really can't stay long. I am working on a case. I just need to take a quick peek at your newspaper's entertainment section."

"Did I ever tell you about the time I auditioned for the role of Cinderella in New York," she asks.

"Yes," I say, smiling through gritted teeth. "You got the part even though you stepped in the cleaning bucket and fell flat on your face on stage."

Mrs. Moore lets out a deep laugh.

"The director was so enamored by how I delivered my lines, he didn't even notice that I fell. And the set director thought my fall was a creative look at Cinderella's character."

"That is so funny, Mrs. Moore. I love hearing about your theater days, but I really just popped by really quick to borrow your newspaper."

"And did I tell you about the time I had to be the star and director because our director quit a week before the show was to start?"

"Yes, I remember that one. Such a great story. If you just tell me where the newspaper is, I'll just grab it really quick and get out of your hair."

"And then there was this other time..."

"Mrs. Moore," I say sharply.

She stops talking and looks intently on me.

"Is Mr. Fluffy Tail feeling well. He looks a bit pale."

Her face grows concerned, as she searches for her beloved cat. I hated to do it, but I really needed her to focus, and she is always worried that one of her five cats are sick or dying.

"I was thinking that earlier today. Maybe I should take him to the vet," she says, talking more to herself than me.

"I'm sure he just needs some extra snuggles. I'll just get that newspaper and let you take care of him."

"Oh, right, the newspaper. I lent it to Mr. Rogers an hour ago."

"Thank you so much! I'll leave these cookies for you and your kitties. See you soon!" I call out and race out the door.

As I closed the door, I heard her start to tell another theater story. I'm not sure if she was talking to me or the cats, but I am just going to assume the cats. I am hot on a case. I can't slow down and lose my steam now.

I knock at Mr. Rogers door, and he answers before I finish knocking. Mr. Rogers is always looking out his door, so I wasn't surprised he answered so quickly.

"Oh, hello, Mr. Rogers. I've come to ask if I can borrow the newspaper Mrs. Moore lent you."

"I'm still reading it," he answers.

"Can I please just borrow the entertainment section?"

"I haven't gotten that far yet," he says.

"But Mr. Rogers, you don't even like the entertainment section. You told me so yourself."

"You're right. I think it is a waste of space."

"So can I borrow it?" I ask.

"I will bring it by when I am done."

"Is that going to be soon? I really need it to figure out something."

"I always finish reading the newspaper at four and take Peanut for a walk at 4:15."

"Okay. I'll be waiting on my porch. Thank you, Mr. Rogers."

I try not to look frustrated as I leave Mr. Rogers house. One thing is for certain. I am never going to get old like Mrs. Moore and Mr. Rogers.

As soon as I reach my house, I check the time. *3:30*. I have to wait another 45 minutes for something I can check in less than a minute.

I pace up and down the yard. The time goes by slower than ever. *What if I carved a hole in Mr. Rogers roof and dropped in and stole the entertainment section?*

I imagine myself all dressed in black, inching slowly from the roof into Mr. Rogers house like I had seen last week in a movie about a jewel thief.

I don't even realize that I am making strange moves or have started doing special ninja-styled kicks and punches. In my head, I am fighting off all of the bad guys that are trying to keep me from getting Mr. Rogers newspaper.

I loud laugh breaks my concentrated thought. I look up and see Owen and Matt on their bikes.

"Careful, Blondie," Owen calls. "You don't want to let the whole neighborhood know your secret ninja skills."

"Nice one," Matt laughs and high-fives Owen.

Boys think anything is funny.

"Oh, hi Mr. Rogers," Owen says respectfully.

"Mr. Rogers!" I yell excitedly and run towards him. "Did you bring the newspaper?"

"Oh, yes, yes. I almost forgot." He slowly unzips his jacket and pulls out the newspaper. "Enjoy."

"Smell ya later, Blondie," Owen calls out as him and Matt race down the sidewalk.

I don't even pay attention to the boys and quickly open up the paper.

I scan the events as quickly as my eyes can until they land on, "Saturday night, 6:30 p.m. Lizzy Lizard at the Epic Center."

"Yes!" I yell and pump my fist.

CHAPTER TWELVE

CONCERT OF CRIME

"Dad!" I exclaim as soon as my dad comes home. "I solved the case."

"Are you sure?" my dad teases, setting his briefcase on the kitchen table.

I lay out all of the clues on the table in front of him, pointing to each one as I say, "We are going to see Lizzy Lizard at the Epic Center Saturday night at six o'clock!" I say excitedly.

"It took you long enough to figure it out," dad laughs.

"Well, I would have figured it out much sooner if I had the Wi-Fi password," I retort.

"Come on, now. That's cheating. Do you think Sherlock Holmes ran to his computer every time he couldn't figure out the answer?"

"I'm sure he would have if he was alive today,"

"Or if he wasn't a fictional character," Jana chimes in.

"Oh hey, Jana, are you coming with us to the concert? Lizzy Lizard is your favorite," I say.

"I never liked Lizzy Lizard. Don't tell people that," she says in an offended voice. She walks off.

I try not to look hurt. Sometimes Jana doesn't say the nicest things. We used to listen to Lizzy Lizard in the pool together and make up synchronized swim routines to her songs.

"Don't take it personally, champ. Sometimes teenagers have a lot of peer pressure at school, and they, unfortunately, take it out on the ones they love the most. I'll have a talk with her," dad says, giving my arm a pat.

"Thanks, dad," I say, still slightly sad.

"And cheer up! We are going to see Lizzy Lizard tomorrow! Aren't you so excited?"

My face breaks out into a huge grin.

"You have no idea," I tell him.

I open my eyes and frantically reach for my glasses on my nightstand. *What time is it? What day is it?*

As soon as I put my glasses on, the room becomes clearer, and I can read the numbers on my digital clock with ease. "7:45," I say out loud. "Phew, I didn't miss the concert."

There is a quiet knock on the door. "Come in," I croak, my voice still not fully awake yet.

"Hi, sweetheart, is everything okay? I heard a lot of banging," my mom says as she peeks her head in the room.

"Everything is fantastic!" I exclaim. "I just had a bad dream that I missed the concert."

"That would be horrible," my mom replies. "Well, since you are up early, how about a little help in the kitchen. I was thinking of making your favorite waffles."

My mouth instantly began to salivate as I imagined shoving a big piece of a chocolate chip waffle in my mouth.

I grumble slightly and lay my head back on the pillow.

"Come on, I know you are too excited to fall back asleep. Plus, it will make the time pass by faster."

Mom was right. I was way too excited to sleep in today. I was already counting down the hours.

I agree and mom says that she will meet me downstairs.

I jump up and start to change my clothes. All I can think about is Lizzy Lizard. The Lizzy Lizard. As in, the best singer in the whole wide world, Lizzy Lizard. I wonder if I could get her autograph. That would be so cool.

What would I say to her? I don't want her to think I am immature or silly. On the other hand, I don't want her to think I don't like her. "I can't believe I get to meet you. You have been my favorite singer since I was 6," I say aloud, in front of the mirror.

Hmm...that might sound too desperate. I look in the mirror and try again, "Oh, hey, Lizzy. I just love your outfit," I say again, trying to sound nonchalant.

I hear a laugh at the door. Jana is standing in the doorway, and she is mocking my movements. "Oh, Lizzy, I am your biggest fan!" she squeals.

"Jana!" I exclaim angrily.

Before I can think of a good comeback, Jana is already down the hall. I can hear her as she runs down the stairs, still laughing.

Sometimes she makes me so angry, I just want to scream. I take a deep breath in, like my mom always tells me to do when I am upset. It doesn't help.

I grab my detective notebook and quickly write in big letters, "I HATE JANA!" I instantly feel better, and I lay the notebook open on my bed, hoping that Jana might see it if she comes back in again. Maybe I should tape it to her door.

I look back at the notebook. The words sure do look angry, and not very nice. I don't really hate Jana. She just makes me mad sometimes.

I think about how I would feel if Jana wrote that about me. It would make me feel horrible. I grab my notebook so that I can rip the page out and destroy it before anyone finds it. Too late.

I hear footsteps and then Jana's head pops into the room, "Blondie, mom wants..."

I follow her eyes to my detective notebook in my hands. She doesn't finish her sentence. Her mouth drops open slightly, and her eyes look sad. She turns and walks towards her room.

"Jana, I didn't mean it," I try to call after her, but she has already run down the hall and shut her door.

Maybe she will just forget about it, kind of like the time she forgot I ruined her favorite sweater by shoving it in my backpack with an open pen.

As I head downstairs, I hear mom humming to the radio. She turns and sees me, "Finally," she exclaims. "Now where did Jana run off to?"

I look at the floor and swirl my toe along the kitchen tile. "Oh, she just had to go to her room for something," I say.

"Blondelle, what happened?" Mom asks accusingly.

How do moms always do that? They always know everything.

"I didn't mean to," I blurt out, holding up my hands.

"Sit and explain," mom says.

I obey even though I would rather hide under my blankets right now. *What have I done? What if my parents won't let me go to the concert now?*

"It's just Jana was making fun of me, and she made me so mad. I wrote, 'I hate Jana,' on my notebook, and she accidentally saw it. But mom, I promise I didn't mean it, I was just mad."

My mom looks at me in silence, arms crossed.

That's it. No Lizzy Lizard for me.

I watch mom walk over to a kitchen drawer and pull out a knife. She holds it up.

Now I am really confused.

"What do you use this for?" mom asks.

"Huh? Um…cutting things?" I answer still confused.

"Exactly. You need a sharp knife to cut your food. It is useful for making meals and eating. However, what happens if you stab someone with this knife?"

"Um, you hurt them?" I am not trying to say everything as a question, but I am so bewildered by what my mom is talking about. Is she really teaching me Knife 101 as a punishment?

"Your words, Blondie, are like knives. They can either be useful and help others, or they can hurt others. How do you want your words to be used?"

"Help others," I answer.

My mom nods. "Why don't you run up and apologize to your sister."

"But mom…" I whine.

"That wasn't a question."

"Can you at least come with me?"

My mom nods and puts her hand on my shoulder.

Once we are in front of Jana's door, I knock softly.

No answer.

I knock again a little harder. "Jana, it's me Blondie. I.."

"Go away!" she interrupts.

"Jana, open up the door, please. Blondie has something very important to say to you."

Mom and I stand in silence for what seems like an eternity. Finally, the door knob turns and opens slightly.

I push on the door gently and see Jana on her bed, face down on her pillow.

My mom pushes me forward into the room.

"Jana, I am really sorry I wrote that. I didn't mean it. I love having you for a sister. It's just that sometimes you get me so mad when you make fun of me."

Jana doesn't move. My mom walks further into the room and sits on her bed.

"Jana, can you sit up please?"

She listens but she doesn't look at either of us.

"Jana, I know Blondie hurt your feelings, but can you look at her and forgive her."

"I forgive you," Jana says monotonously.

"Jana, is there something else bothering you?" my mom asks.

"No," Jana says, but as she says it a tear falls from her eye.

"Come on, Jana. You can tell us."

Jana bites her lip, and then quietly says, "I am just jealous that Blondie gets to go to the Lizzy Lizard concert." A few more tears fall from her eyes.

Am I hearing things correctly? Jana is jealous of me. I thought she hated Lizzy Lizard.

My mom lets out a chuckle. "Oh, Jana. Dad and I asked if you wanted to go, and you said Lizzy Lizard was, and I quote, 'lame sauce'."

"I know. That's what all my friends say, but she is still my favorite singer. I just didn't want them to make fun of me."

"Anyone that makes fun of Lizzy Lizard is lame sauce!" I shout.

"Thank you, Blondie," my mom says. "And Jana, your little sister has a point. You shouldn't worry about what others think of you. You are your own unique person with special talents, likes, and dislikes. If someone doesn't want to be friends with you because you like Lizzy Lizard, then maybe they aren't a friend worth having."

Jana nods but still looks down.

"I've got an idea," I say. "Jana can have my ticket."

"What?" Jana exclaims, looking instantly happier. "But then you wouldn't be able to go."

My mom holds up her hand. "Blondie, that is very sweet of you to offer, but I can't let you do that."

"Yeah," Jana adds in. "It's my fault that I said no."

"Thankfully your mom knows you better than you know yourself, Jana," my mom adds.

"What do you mean?" Jana asks.

"Well, I told your dad to get an extra ticket just in case because I had a feeling," mom smiles.

Jana throws her arms around my mom's neck. "Thank you! Thank you!" she exclaims.

I pump my fist in the area. "This is going to be so awesome!"

As my dad drives off the freeway, I can already see the crowd of cars formed in front of the Epic Center.

"Can you believe it," I say, turning to my sister. "Lizzy Lizard is within a mile of us. I have never been so close to a superstar before!"

"Just wait until you see where your seats are, then you will really be excited" my dad chimes in.

Jana and I look at each other, both trying hard not to squeal in excitement.

Dad was right. Jana and I squealed when he showed us our seats. "VIP seats for my two very important people," Dad laughs.

I knew dad worked at the Epic Center, but his job is in safety. I always thought his job was boring, and even the days I visited him in the office, it seemed like all he did was sit at his desk. I had no idea that he got to actually see celebrities.

"This is the best day ever," I squeal, giving my dad a tight hug.

"And after the concert, we get to go backstage and meet Miss Lizard," my dad adds.

"What!?" Jana screams. She can no longer pretend she is too cool to be here. She is just as excited as me.

"Do you think she will let me have her autograph?" I ask.

"I bet she will," my dad answers.

We sit down in our seats and watch the opening act. It was a boy band from Britain that I had never heard of. All of the girls in the crowd screamed, but not me. I was saving my voice for Lizzy Lizard.

The whole arena went pitch black except for two bright spotlights that pointed to the stage.

"Here she comes," I exclaim as I hold on tightly to my dad's arm.

"Alright, who's ready to party?" Lizzy Lizard's voice comes booming out of all the speakers. The crowd goes wild. I can see her blonde, curly hair and sequin outfit as she starts walking towards the front of the stage.

"Then let's put our hands..." Lizzy's voice cuts off as she falls to the floor with a loud thud. Screams fill the audience and a lot of confused voices fill the air. The band members raced over towards her.

"Stay here!" dad yells as he pulls out a walkie-talkie that was hidden in his jacket.

"Team, we have an emergency situation. Lizzy is down. Security get ready to escort all individuals out. Accident management team, we need all hands on, call emergency services and keep the crowd calm. I'm going to make an announcement," my dad shouts into his walkie-talkie.

He makes his way on stage and bends down to say something to the band members who are huddled over Lizzy. He then takes the microphone and faces the crowd.

My dad has always said he has stage fright, so it was a complete shock when he spoke so confidently in front of the thousands of people in the Epic Center.

"Attention, please. We are sorry to inform you that the concert will be postponed tonight. Lizzy Lizard is ill and has fainted, but she will be all right. We are going to get her to the hospital now. On behalf of the Epic Center, we apologize for this inconvenience. You will be contacted in the next few business days in regards to rescheduling your show or receiving a full refund."

The Epic Center started filling up with people shouting questions and other words I could not make out.

"I know you are all worried and upset by the events tonight, but in order for us to do our job and get Lizzy the care she needs, we need you to leave in an orderly fashion. Security guards will help guide you to the doors. All bathrooms except the one in the main lobby have been closed, and we will be guiding you out through the main lobby. Thank you for your cooperation."

Just then the lights on the stage went black while the lights on the audience brighten. Someone with bright pink hair darts behind the stage.

"Did you see that," I ask Jana.

Jana's mouth is wide open and her eyes are glued to the spot where the pink-haired lady disappeared.

"That's Myra," she says hoarsely. "She was just standing in front of us."

"Which means I don't think Lizzy Lizard's accident was an accident after all," I say.

To be continued...

Thank you so much for reading! If you enjoyed this book, please share it with a friend and leave a review. Your review doesn't need to be long, just a few words. http://amzn.to/2itvpsa

Keep reading for a sneak peek at the next book in the Blondie McGhee series. Coming February 2017.

Pressure To Perform

Excerpt

Well, my dream has finally come true. But instead of being within arms distance of my all-time favorite singer, Lizzy Lizard, I am standing next to the spot she passed out thirty minutes before. So much for a concert.

` Since dad is in charge of safety, he has kicked into high gear. I've never seen him in action before. I just thought he had a boring desk job.

"Alright, all Epic Center staff and volunteers, you are expected to stay until the police have taken your statement. If you are missing when it's your turn for questioning, consider yourself on the top of the suspect list and looking for a new job for due diligence. "

This is what happens when my dad watches too many shows about cops and lawyers. He starts using "suspect" and "due diligence" in the same sentence.

"Dad, is everything going to be all right?" I ask when he breaks away from the other Epic Center employees.

My dad ran his hand through his hair and exhaled deeply.

"Don't worry, kiddo. It will all be fine. I'll call your mom to come and get you. "

"No, please don't. I can help you." I beg.

"Sweetheart, that is very sweet, and normally I would love your pro detective skills, but tonight there is a lot at stake. I need to get this mess settled and find the cause behind this tonight before the press run the story tomorrow."

"Dad, are they going to fire you?" Jana asks.

"What? No, that's not fair. It's not your fault!" I scream.

"Calm down, calm down," my dad says in a hushed voice waving his hands downward.

"But you said they fired the guy before you because he made a big mistake," Jana adds.

My dad sighs heavily.

"Girls, please don't worry about that..." My dad starts to say but is quickly interrupted by a woman wearing a headset and three different walkie-talkies on her waistband.

He puts a finger up to show he will be right with her and then turns to us.

"Take my cell phone and call your mom to get you. Also, tell her that if she needs to get ahold of me, call me on my work cell. Though please let her know that things are a bit in crisis mode right now, so only call if it's crucial. Okay?"

Jana and I nod, and Jana takes the phone out of my dad's hand.

"And no texting your friends, Jana," my dad warns quickly.

"Okay, okay," Jana replies but my dad is already in a conversation with the headset lady. They are both talking angrily with a lot of hand movements.

Jana throws herself in a nearby seat and scrolls through my dad's cell phone. "Where did all those games go?" she asks, not looking up.

Without waiting for an answer, Jana sits up and says, "I guess I should just call mom. "

"No!" I blurt out. A few Epic workers glance over but then quickly go back to what they were doing.

"It's just if you call mom then she will pick us up and we will have to go to bed."

"And?" My sister asks, looking slightly annoyed.

"Don't you want to help dad?"

"Um, I guess, but there isn't much we can do," she answers.

"That's what you think. I packed my emergency detective kit," I say showing her my backpack.

"What? I thought you told dad you packed snacks for the concert," Jana points out.

"Well, I did, but my main purpose was to make sure my detective kit was packed."

Jana nods with a smirk on her face.

"Well, it's a good thing I did. Now we can solve the case and save dad's job," I say, still trying to convince her not to call mom.

Look for the newest Blondie McGhee book on Amazon early 2017.

Made in the USA
San Bernardino, CA
18 November 2018